A Note to Parents

Reading books aloud and playing word games are two valuable ways parents can help their children learn to read. The easy-to-read stories in the **My First Hello Reader! With Flash Cards** series are designed to be enjoyed together. Six activity pages and 16 flash cards in each book help reinforce phonics, sight vocabulary, reading comprehension, and facility with language. Here are some ideas to develop your youngster's reading skills:

Reading with Your Child

- Read the story aloud to your child and look at the colorful illustrations together. Talk about the characters, setting, action, and descriptions. Help your child link the story to events in his or her own life.
- Read parts of the story and invite your child to fill in the missing parts. At first, pause to let your child "read" important last words in a line. Gradually, let your child supply more and more words or phrases. Then take turns reading every other line until your child can read the book independently.

Enjoying the Activity Pages

- Treat each activity as a game to be played for fun. Allow plenty of time to play.
- Read the introductory information aloud and make sure your child understands the directions.

Using the Flash Cards

- Read the words aloud with your child. Talk about the letters and sounds and meanings.
- Match the words on the flash cards with the words in the story.
- Help your child find words that begin with the same letter and sound, words that rhyme, and words with the same ending sound.
- Challenge your child to put flash cards together to make sentences from the story and create new sentences.

Above all else, make reading time together a fun time. Show your child that reading is a pleasant and meaningful activity. Be generous with your praise and know that, as your child's first and most important teacher, you are contributing immensely to his or her command of the printed word.

—Tina Thoburn, Ed.D.
Educational Consultant

For Amy—who pulled through them all.

Library of Congress Cataloging-in-Publication Data

Hall, Kirsten.
A bad, bad day / by Kirsten Hall ; illustrated by Laura Rader.
p. cm. — (My first hello reader!)
"With flash cards."
Summary: A young boy's day starts badly, but his mood improves when his teacher gives him a good mark on his paper.
ISBN 0-590-25496-0
[1. Mood (Psychology)—Fiction. 2. Schools—Fiction. 3. Stories in rhyme.]
I. Rader, Laura, ill. II. Title. III. Series.
PZ8.3.H146Bad 1995
[E]—dc20

94-39148
CIP
AC

24 23 22 21 20 19 18 17 16 15 14 8 9/9 0/0

Printed in the U.S.A. 24
First Scholastic printing, September 1995

A BAD, BAD DAY

by Kirsten Hall

Illustrated by Laura Rader

My First Hello Reader!
With Flash Cards

SCHOLASTIC INC.

New York Toronto London Auckland Sydney

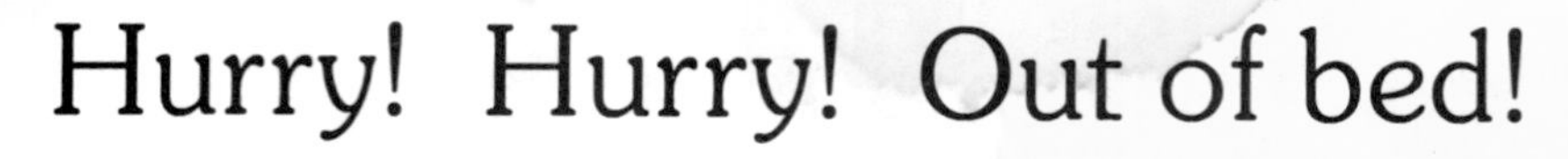
Hurry! Hurry! Out of bed!

Hurry!

Ouch, I hit my head!

Out my window, I see gray.

What a day.

A bad, bad day.

Hurry! Hurry!
I am late!

Where's my breakfast?

I can't wait.

I spilled my breakfast.

I can't fuss.

Hurry! Hurry!
There's the bus!

A bad, bad day.

We'll take the car!

What a day!

I got a star!

My Bad, Bad Day

Did you ever have a bad, bad day?

Tell about it.

What made it bad?

Rhyming Words

Rhyming words sound alike. The words **plus** and **bus** are rhyming words. For each word on the left, point to the rhyming word on the right.

fuss	wait
gray	bus
late	bed
head	day

Feelings

People's faces can show what they are feeling. There are two faces next to each word below. Point to the face that goes with the word.

What's Next?

Look at each picture. Tell what you think might happen next.

Opposites

Opposites are words that mean something completely different. **Big** and **little** are opposites.

Look at the words below. In each row, point to the word that means the opposite of the first word.

good	large	bad	silly
early	late	wrong	right
in	never	over	out
can	always	can't	funny

A Good, Good Day

Make up a story about a good, good day. Add as many good things as you can!

Answers

(*My Bad, Bad Day*)

Answers will vary.

(*Rhyming Words*)

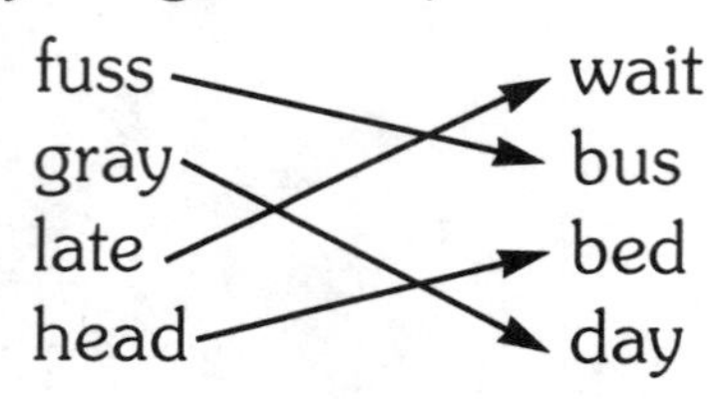

(*Feelings*)

(*What's Next?*)

The plates might fall and break.
The water in the sink might overflow.
The hamster might get out of the cage.

(*Opposites*)

good	large	bad	silly
early	late	wrong	right
in	never	over	out
can	always	can't	funny

(*A Good, Good Day*)

Answers will vary.